Bear Woke Up

Written and Illustrated by:

ISBN: 978-163578-000-0
Printed and bound in the United States
First Edition

Current contact information for Karl Steam can be found at
www.karlsteam.com

To my children,
with love.

A bird was singing when Bear woke up. He was under his favorite tree, the one with a root that could be used as a pillow.

Bear was hungry. He went to the meadow and was lucky enough to find some blueberries. They were his favorite.

The cool water felt good,
until the wind began to blow.

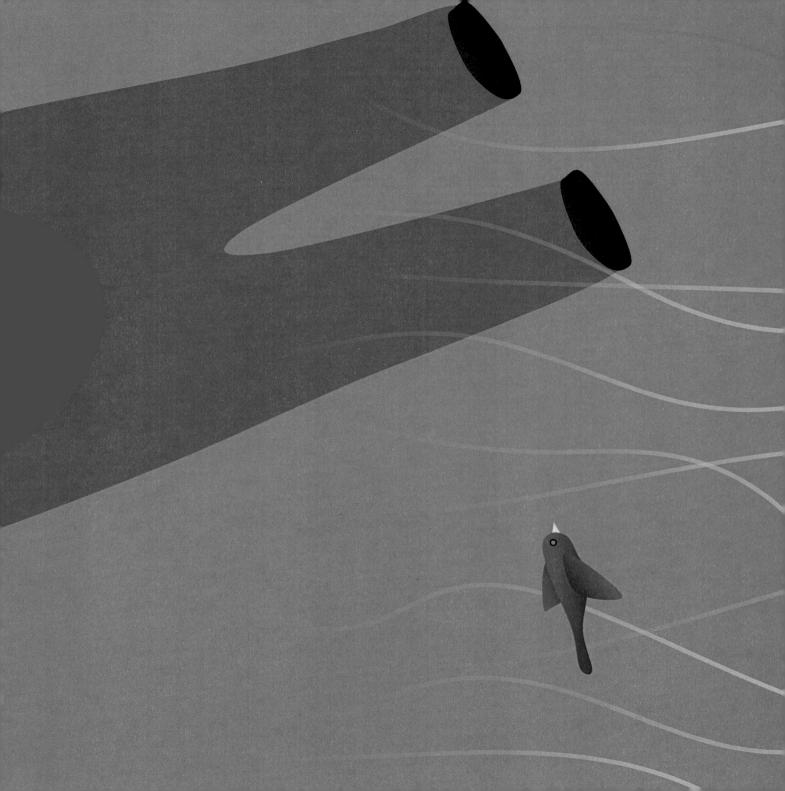

Waves formed, and Bear had to get out of the lake. At least the wind would help his fur to dry quickly.

Bear noticed that pine needles were blowing off the trees. He filled his paw with grass and watched them scatter through the air.

Bear danced when he felt raindrops falling. He twirled and waved his arms until he became tired.

Bear went back to his favorite tree. The ground was flooded, so he decided to look for a different tree to rest under...

and wondered if he could find a
new one that he'd like even better.

KARL STEAM.com

Karl Steam is the author of *How Santa Changed* and the novel *Purple Pup*. More stories are being prepared for publishing, so look online for an updated list.

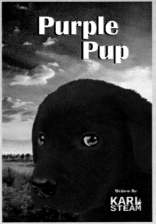

Give yourself a break,
and let Karl do the teaching.

Viewable at youtube.com or www.karlsteam.com

Instructional videos
and activity sheets
are available online.

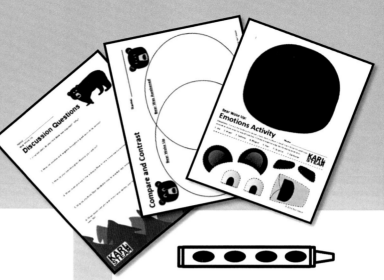

Discussion Questions

1. In which story do you think Bear
was happiest? Why?

2. How did positive and negative
thoughts impact each of the
stories?

3. How do your own thoughts
influence your actions?

4. What could you say to the
unhappy Bear to help it view each
circumstance differently?

5. Why do you think Bear decided
to look for another tree in one
story, and not the other?

6. What lesson can you learn from
these stories, and how can it be
applied to your own life?

Classroom Activities

1. Brainstorm situations that are
usually seen as being unpleasant.
As a class or in small groups, think of
something good about each
situation.

2. Us a Venn Diagram to compare
and contrast the stories.

3. Print the Bear Emotions Activity
Sheet, and experiment with the
ways eyebrow positioning can
portray Bear's different emotions.

4. Write two stories using the same
events, but give the character in one
story a positive attitude and the
character in the other story a
negative attitude.

Bear tried to sleep, but he kept thinking about how long it would take for the water to move away from his tree.

Bear went back to his favorite tree.
The ground was flooded, so he
roared until he became tired.

It started to rain. Bear lowered his head. He had just dried off, and now his fur was wet again.

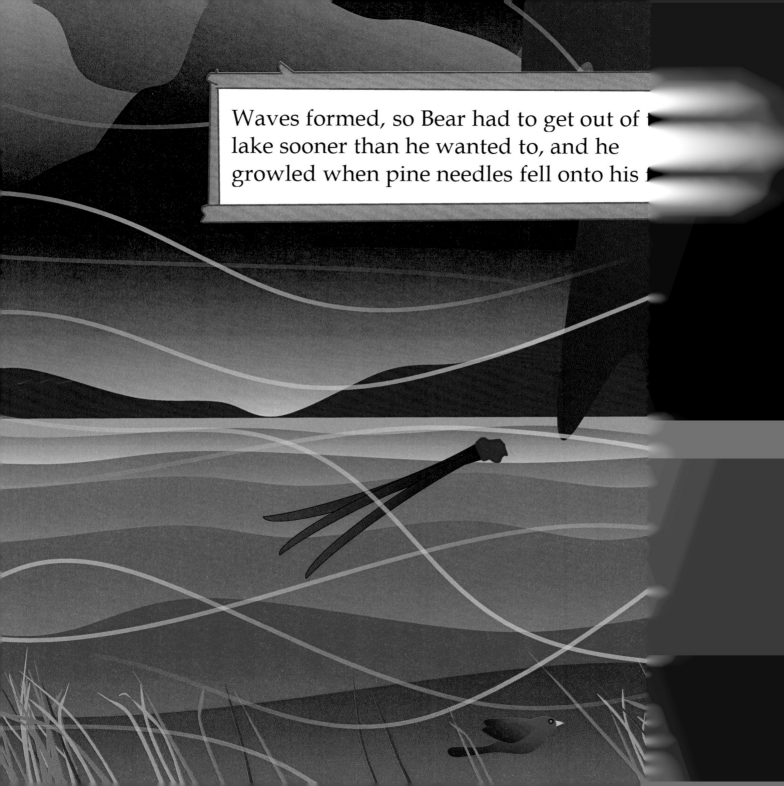

Waves formed, so Bear had to get out of the lake sooner than he wanted to, and he growled when pine needles fell onto his f

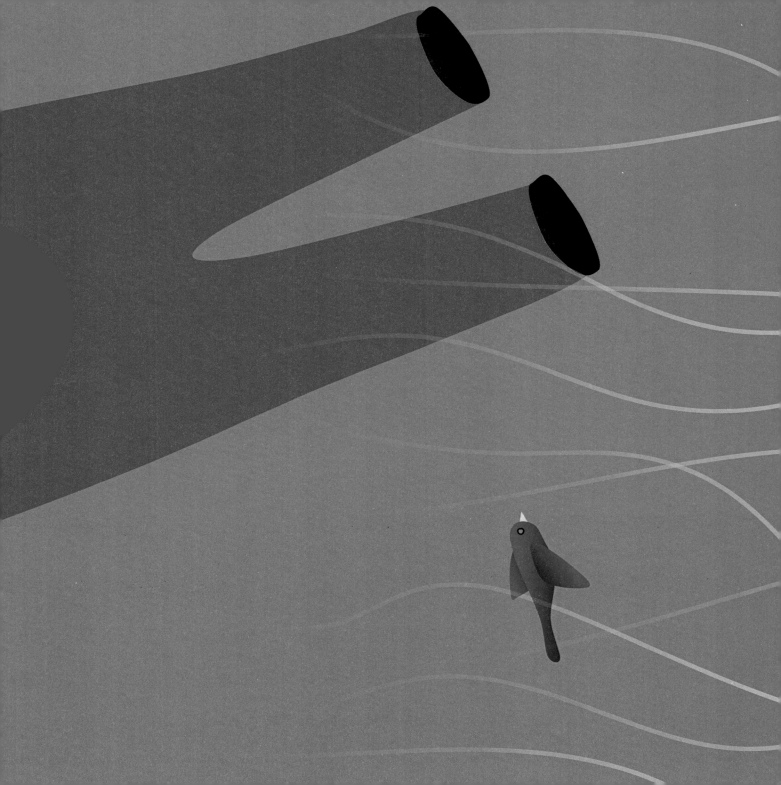

It was a hot afternoon, and Bear had to walk all the way back to the lake to cool off.

Bear was starving. He went to the meadow, but mostly found red berries. Bear hated red berries.

Bear was awakened by a loud bird. He had been resting under his favorite tree, the one with a root that could be used as a pillow.

Bear Was Awakened

Written and Illustrated by:

Made in the USA
San Bernardino, CA
21 December 2016